Books for Boys

Lost Campers

By

My books are a project to get my son to enjoy reading. The stories use early reading words and subject matter young boys like. The words in the book range from pre-primer through third grade words. Early readers will find reading and learning more enjoyable because of the appropriate and interesting content.

For all boys who find reading
boring!

Making Reading Fun!

Lost Campers

The long ride was easy; it was walking to our campsite that was hard. We had to go over a long bridge to get to our favorite spot in the woods.

We found our spot deep in the woods around five o'clock at night. We were all hot and wanted a cold drink of water. We'd had to carry our bags all the way to camp.

We put up a red tent, a grey tent, and a blue tent. It was a lot of work. It is funny how some work is fun and some work is not fun. This was fun work.

We had to find lots of logs to make a fire for the night. Together we all sat around the camp fire to sing some songs, laugh at funny jokes, and tell some stories.

It must have been around three in the morning when I woke up.

I had to go into the woods to go to the bathroom. I went so far away from the camp I could not find my way back. Something moved by a tree and made me jump. My foot hit a rock and I feel into the water.

I grabbed a log and floated down the river.

On my right side was a big brown bear. He took a swing at me. He missed. I said, "Better luck next time!" Just then I heard a loud noise.

My log went around a bend, in the river and I could see a waterfall.

I grabbed hold of a branch. Just as I took hold of the branch, my log went over the falls. I had a rope and tied it to the tree. I was able to swing to the other side of the water and jump to safety.

I almost hit a bee hive with my foot. When I let go of my rope it flew back and hit the bee hive.

I had to run fast. I saw a cave and went inside. The bees did not see me, and I said, "Better luck next time!"

I knew I was pretty close to our camp. I just did not know which way to go.

Six wolves came down the hill barking and barking.

I ran right at them and jumped into a tree as their white fangs almost bit my behind. I said, "Better luck next time!"

I jumped from tree to tree. Finally I climbed down a vine and jumped off onto the ground.

Once I got down I saw my friend. He asked, "Where have you been? You should get some eggs before they get cold."

THE END

Keep Reading!